For my parents…

STRANGE EUCHARIST:

A Diverse Collection of 3 Short Stories

by

Ralph Anthony Freda

ISBN10: 0578606593

ISBN: 978-0-578-60659-0

THE BREAK ROOM

By Ralph Freda

The thing I'm most aware of is how my eyes sting–seem dry–at this time of the morning... I work the paint department–a common stock boy–at Builders Mart. A cup of coffee from McDonald's picked me up, but the ephemeral fuzzy buzz is gone and I close my eyes, a wave of warmth behind them goes on forever to the back of my head; and I'm tempted to fall asleep, right there on my feet.

Mr. Persky is there, dutifully, at five-thirty a.m., so we can be open by 6. Most of us are there, in the parking lot, waiting in our cars for no more than five minutes, before he pulls up in his outdated shitbox economy car. He gets out–a powerful little man, walking quickly, wordlessly, to the front doors of the building. (Sometimes he twirls keys, hung from the end of a long, rubber, spring-thingy keychain; sometimes not.) We all get out of our cars, and silently follow Mr. Persky to the front doors like condemned goslings. Some of us nod a half-awake 'hello'–mostly the guys who have been here the longest. I have very little in common with these kids, and even less to say; so I am always wordless. I look at Mr. Persky, and feel sorry for him–he can't be more than thirty-five; already roped and tied with two kids, and a twenty-year mortgage... Builder's Mart used to be Builder's World, not five years ago, and the chances that *this* place will go out of business is great; and I can see when I look at him this is something he tries not to think about all the time...

Six or seven of us walk into the cavernous wholesale building–it isn't yet lit, and cold Mr. Persky runs, keys jingling violently, to shut the alarm off in forty-five seconds. As he's manager, Builder's Mart has entrusted him with the secret code.... We go to the cold, stark, depressing break room; each of us putting on a Navy blue Builder's Mart smock, that's about as ugly as my mother's ass. Carolyn, a seventeen year old beauty with cinnamon freckles, and a long thick head of red hair, is next to me...

"Hi, Ronny" she says, and I'm grateful for this.

"Hey, Carolyn," I reply, trying to sound firm and cool, and leave it at that. She's not the sole female employee; but she's the only young girl, who works with all us guys in the morning. I don't know her that well–don't know *why* she works at seventeen, instead of going to high school–but she knows practically everything about hardware, and more than once I have embarrassedly dragged a customer over to her with a question ... I feel sensitive to the fact that she works with a bunch of young, immature guys; so I always try to take care with her...

Fifteen minutes later, I am stocking shelves, and seriously considering treating myself to a fourth, or fifth (I've lost count) five-second nap on my feet; but, really, I think I'm addicted to the warm, almost burning sensation that occurs when I close my eyes within the cold store and try not to think on this, as it will cause me to be unable to stop.

I attain a perfectly therapeutic silence, save for an occasional clunk, created by the gallon-cans, and I see a shadowy figure walking less than gracefully toward me–I know it's Betty, my department manager; also the second and only other female to work with us, morning shift. The only time she speaks to me–ever–is to inform me I've done something wrong, or ask whether or not I'm informed about such and such a product... She is a portly woman, with older-woman ivory skin white against a head of reddish hair that looks more like a wig.

She lifts her thick-framed asshole glasses, farther up the bridge of her asshole nose; holds them steady with two asshole fingers, and says, "I notice the shelves of the Glidden semi-gloss weren't faced..."

'Faced', is when you bring every individual unit of a product to the very front edge of a shelf–the idea being, a customer, deciding upon this product, finds it accessible, and isn't dissuaded by actually having to reach... Supermarkets have guys like me running all over the place, making sure their products are easy to reach. We learned about the psychology of product placement, and the omni-importance of such things, from a video tape shown in the break room. In three separate viewings, ultimately thirty of us spent an hour and a half of unpaid time, to be instructed of the wondrous worlds of eye-level shelf placement, facing, and turning products so the label faces the consumer...

I have my answer ready for her. "I don't know *why*, Betty—everything was done when I turned it over to Carey." Carey is the kid, about my age, who relieves me at 2:30, afternoon shift. It's a bullshit game we play; the legacy of America, really—it's called, passing the buck.

She looks at me evenly, silently; and has since brought her hand down from her face. It isn't simply that she knows I'm full of shit...she knows that *I* know she knows I'm full of shit so we're on dangerous ground, here... Betty is paint department manager, and following all her years, probably knows more about paint than any other living being.

"Yeah... We have to watch, because of the Glidden people..." The paint company giant is forever sending moles to the stores, to make sure their product is appropriately, if not prominently displayed... She has said this to me in an almost confidential manner, and I feel a guilty tinge, because she is unaware I loathe her.

One long look at Betty—in fact, one look at anybody in this place—and my enthusiasm for pursuit of a college education intensified... The Navy has a term for people who opt out of the rat-race of life—basically hang in there, until they die—and that term is 'lifer'; in there for life... Builder's World had more than one lifer within its shallow body, especially at this ungodly hour... It's my third year of junior college; working toward my AA, with an emphasis on business. I took a year off, following high school graduation—still live at home—and the people here remind me not to be too fond of taking years off, either ...

Now it's just past 6:00 a.m., and being the month of November, the sun is coming up; so, at this time, three mornings a week, I leave the paint aisle, and look fifty yards ahead, through the front doors–the sky is a sickly light blue, a tired slave of an incomprehensible sun, that will soon establish itself, fiercely... The cars that are going by, on the main street, are more now than were present in the total darkness of 5:15 a. m. All these people, barely out of bed–half of them, showered, and heads still wet– spending another day, blindly obedient to the circumstances that be... I imagine them– almost see them–eyes pried wide open, as if by force, much like myself, barely two hours ago...

Finally, it's 10:30; fifteen minutes, until break time. We've had one customer all day; some weary looking, slight-framed guy, with head of thin curly hair, and glasses. He wants my expertise, about what I 'would recommend'–satin finish, or semi-gloss... He says his wife is leaving it up to him, and swallowing my disbelief that someone would marry this guy, I bite back the urge to blurt out that I 'recommend' *me* going back into bed with his wife; though, whoever would marry this guy, leaves me dubious, skeptical.

Moreover, he wants his bathroom a sort of beige; so, it's up to me to produce it for him. I grab a gallon of semi-gloss (the pick, of my expertise), and ask him to follow me to the color mixing machine. It's a contraption that resembles an octopus–black metal, for the most part, with a series of ten horizontal arms jutting from it, all around. The arms are really levers, each one representing a tint. You put the can of white–which is your basic color–beneath the lever that distributes your tint. Pull the lever straight out, toward you, according to the amount of tint, and release into the can of white. Of course, with each of the ten levers, containing different colors, the combinations produce hundreds of finished colors.

"Okay," I say to him. "We just have to mix."

The thing is, after pointing out which particular beige he wanted, he has stood almost immediately close, beside me, saying nothing; not one word, even following my mentioning the mixing process...   The mixer resembles medieval torture device–you place the can diagonally into the contraption, secure it–always, always, always, secure it, Betty implores me, begs of me, almost; else you have unmixed paint everywhere... Flip a switch; and...voila! A minute of violent, controlled shaking, and your paint is ready.

I hand him the can. He thanks me, forcing a smile, that he believes is necessary, but ends up, half-hearted, and pathetic, and I watch him go back out, into the world.

By now, fifteen minutes have passed. It's break time; and of course Betty ambles over to me–she's fresh off her break–and I feel the oxygen rushing out of the world, the closer she gets...

"He get what he wanted?" she asks, of the skinny guy.

"Yeah," I try to be as bland as possible. "Semi-gloss. Beige." I stand, fascinated by her being so on top of mundane things.

She pivots her short, portly body around, slowly, surveying the large, relatively quiet and empty warehouse–she looks like a hostile gun turret from a science-fiction story.

"Quiet today," she says, definitely of the obvious, and I remain silent, no longer feeling obligated–or a desire–to speak.

Betty then proceeds to say to me, what she has, each day we have worked together for two years. "You can take your break.

"I look at her, and say my usual, two years running. "Okay."

I head through the opening leading to the back of the store, and there is a fantasy in the back of mind, that I shall never again see the Paint Department; that it will most simply, and silently vanish; Betty along with, holding fast to the paint mixer; which will only reinforce my would-be admiration for her; her dedication to all things paint...

But, probably not today...

The actual break room is a stark white (though dulled and dirtied, over time). The entire ceiling is translucent plastic panels, beneath which are fluorescent, white lighting tubes; and when no one's in here, they produce a dutiful, buzzing sound. The light in this room is unnaturally stark, ugly, especially when you know it's broad daylight outside... I think the point behind this–coupled with the absence of windows–is to remind the slaves they exist within a bleak and meaningless life...

The only things of color–even remotely suggesting cheer–are the soda machines, candy and chip machines, and blue employee lockers, which are small enough to be stacked, three at a time, in a row of five... The refrigerator is a stark, yet somehow hideous white, as the room.

There are three people, already there, as I walk in.

Carolyn is there, in a chair, tipped back against the wall, feet dangling, from the floor. I'm grateful she's there–I have an enormous crush on her, and each time she opens her mouth, to speak, I fear she will mention she's leaving the job. She and I make eye contact.

"Hey," she says, to me, sweeping her red blonde hair aside, with one hand, holding a Coke in the other.

"Hey, Carolyn," I say, for the second time today.

Woody is there, seated at the table in the center of the room... Woody works in lumber (the gag being his name is Woody) –he's in his mid-thirties; an on-again, off- again junkie, whose relapses has caused him to miss weeks at a time. The only reason he hasn't been fired, is that he knows everything about lumber, and could never be replaced... The few times we have covered for him, we had no idea what we were doing, and were almost killed (at the very least, lost a limb), in the process.

Woody has a long face-accented by a thick, black moustache-that is absolutely demure, tired of everything. His eyes lock onto mine, and he nods, wordlessly, as always.

Also at the table is Brian, from Gardening... I hate to say this, but Brian is precisely what I want to avoid becoming in life–he is twenty-three, already married, and has two kids a home... He constantly rattles on, to anyone within earshot, about how rough his life is.

A week after I turned twenty-one, he convinced me to follow him to a nearby bar for a couple of beers–this was something I was not quite ready for. I figured it best if we took his car; left mine here, in the parking lot... He drove wordlessly to the bar; cigarette clenched between two knuckles of his driving hand; some classic rock station playing archaic stuff on the radio... It seemed to me he had some intense, inner monologue going through his head and I had to constantly suppress a premonition that he would suddenly turn the wheel, steering us into oncoming traffic.

What followed was worse...

We pulled up at a local dive called Marty's. Dark as midnight inside; the brightest light, at the far end, leading to the restroom, of which there was only one. A jukebox had a selection of sleazy bar music–slightly dated–for a clientele that tried desperately to believe they were still twenty years younger than they were. Dartboards, some electronic, hung alongside one another, under dim, sickly, yellow bulbs.

There was the obligatory sour smell of spilled beer; and behind the bar were the usual two rows of bottles, probably half-diluted with tap water... This keeps the drinks below 2.50 for well 3.50 for call.

I realized, then and there, that Brian was a regular in this place– there were two other people at the bar; and the bartender–a woman– all of whom he knew by name... I took a seat next to him, mildly in shock, at the idea of this twenty-three year old kid sitting in a dark bar, whiling away his time, and wishing away the world...

I had a beer, bottled... Brian had beer, in a glass; then another, then another; and chain-smoking, chain-smoking... I realized, what

he was doing, was avoiding going home, one beer at a time... By
his third beer, I had pretty much the story of his life–Got his girlfriend
pregnant when he was eighteen; *she* was seventeen. Her family
disowned her, and he had no family to speak of... Now, five years
later, they have a total of two kids–both boys–and are cramped in a
small, one-room apartment... According to him, his young wife can't
cook; and more than two, three meals a week are frozen lasagna for
four... The other three are Kentucky Fried Chicken...

"Fuckin,"... he begins, blowing smoke through his nose; and he
looks like some despondent dragon. "I lost it, once or twice...
Came home... the kids shit all over the place... Fuckin'... frozen food
in the oven... I went off..."

He goes silent again, back to his beer; and I am terribly sad for
this guy; this guy I have known for two years, and whose life I never
cared to know, in just such a way...

Over the course of the next hour–I went through two beers; he,
two mixed drinks (each with adjoining beer), and probably five
cigarettes–he went on to tell me that these incidents of domestic
abuse have occurred before; that they were more *recurring*, than
occurring...

He and I sat in this dark bar, two of five people in the place
(including Judy, the barmaid) –three o'clock in the afternoon, mind
you–and suddenly, I pictured clearly, his young wife, whose name I
blissfully knew not... This poor girl–herself barely twenty- one–
going through life; toting three kids; living in sub-standard conditions;
barely above the poverty line; and married to *this* guy, going from
drab dreary; waiting for the kids to come of school age, at which time
she will get a part-time job...

And married to Brian, I bet everything that if this girl partied
once a month, it was a miracle... I borrowed one of his cigarettes, and
counted my blessings in silence...

Finally, after a thick five minute stretch of being silent, he turned to look at me... "You ready...? he asked. I had been aching for these words five minutes after we walked in the door.

"Sure," I drawled slowly, trying to be nonchalant; blowing it by instantly hopping off the bar stool...

When we thrust open the door of the place, sunlight from everywhere flooded my eyes... I was never so aware of contrast in my life; and realized suddenly, that this was very much a part of this guy's life; five days a week, immediately following work, he came to this desperate Disneyland–a young, vital man–and sat next to the lonely, dilapidated people, endlessly pouring cheap, watered down alcohol down their throats.

He avoided going home, one beer at a time...

The drive back to Builder's Mart, and to my car, is surreal–Brian is more tense now than when we first set out on this excursion... He's driving with one hand atop the wheel; his grip is hard, he knuckles are white. A cigarette burns down, squeezed tight between his fingers. The alcohol has made him silent; intensely so; and not one word was said between us the whole way back... I was regretful of the decision to have done this with my afternoon... I was forced to look into the world of this cool, seemingly together guy from work, and was saddened by the desperation of what I saw...

I would decline future invitations...

Now, sitting in the break room, Brian busied himself by devouring a bologna sandwich... Everyone kept their lunches in their locker, either in brown bags, or lunchboxes–apparently, lunch hours are an optimum time to visit your doctor, and several stool samples, in brown paper bags (and specimen cups, of course), had been discovered on a shelf in the break room fridge.... That was one conversation that went 'round, for a very long time.

Woody, who had his face buried in the 'Easy Crosswords' paperback, stopped twiddling his pencil in frustration. "A mineral found in red meat... Four letters..." This meant someone had to come to his aid. Without missing a beat, Carolyn, looking down at her own book, offered, "Iron."

"That's pretty good..." Woody assimilated the answer, filled the boxes accordingly. "Hows come you know that?"

Carolyn looked up, a bit intensely, from switching her focus from reading. Her face was young, ivory, and beautiful. "My kid is iron poor," she said evenly. "I have to know shit like that..."

The mention of her kid was a revelation to me... I never knew. She was always this young girl–beautiful, long reddish blonde hair; beautiful, tight little body; smart as anything–who came and went, five days a week; saying very little to me, and anyone else, around here, for that matter... Now, she was a young mother (whether she was married or not, I didn't know), with an inner life, that was extraordinary...

"You have a kid?!" These words just shot out of my mouth… I think this was the most serious I had ever addressed her; certainly a departure from the 'Hey', and 'What's goin' on?' of our usual encounters.

This girl, who I had known–albeit casually–for three years; lasciviously longed for; lusted after (once while drunk, and trying to fall asleep)–my mysterious, cinnamon- blonde Heavy Metal goddess–was a seventeen-year-old working mother... This girl, with a half-empty can of Coca-Cola between her dangling feet, and a half-empty bag of Fritos in her hand... was a young, unwed (as far as I knew) mother.

She looked at me evenly; spoke in an even, lower tone... "Two years old... Name's Jessica..." She looked after me a second longer, then went back to her Fritos. Anybody who experienced what I did would've thought her barely perceptible low tone, and the barely perceptible, cold, sharp delivery of her words, were the ones of a defensive mother of a three-year-old... But I saw it; and I knew– they were feelings conveyed of a bright seventeen-year-old, worn prematurely down–with a back, prematurely sore–in shit, go-nowhere job; beneath a sky of sickly, neon lights... I saw the resentment she bore for her child; the frustration; possibly even hostility... Everyone else her age was spending their lunch-hour smoking excellent dope; getting loaded in the school parking lot; while she was answering questions, about what hammer to use, what spackle is best...

I knew not to go any further; that my prying into something, of which I knew not a thing wasn't appreciated... I watched her for a moment, and thought to myself that I would never consider her quite the same way...

I went to the vending machine to get my usual break time fix–a package of two large 'soft batch' cookies, kept soft for up to two years through the help of chemicals approved by the FDA. A picture of a little old lady was upon every package–be they oatmeal or chocolate chip–and the consumer was supposed to believe the little lady was their concerned, loving grandmother... I think the chemicals are addictive–I swear I can taste them; and five minutes following consumption, feel mildly the effects, the way a smoker would their fourth or fifth cigarette of the day...

Sitting back down, my thoughts focused soberly upon my immediate surroundings... I stole quick looks of assessment of the three people I had known for the better part of two years, realizing I didn't know anything about them...

Carolynn was in a predicament for quite a while... Unless she married well– some guy willing to put a roof over her and her daughter's heads... But the way you meet such a guy is to socialize, and I don't think she had the time, or the means, for such things... Her other option was an education, and again, the issue was time... I attend school part-time, but I live at home, so I work only part-time. Carolyn worked here full time, so I'm assuming her daughter and she had a place of their own...

Across the table from me, Brian was finishing his sandwich... I clearly saw him at Builder's Mart (provided the place stayed in business) for the next twenty years–his wife and kids had him land·locked, devoting his waking hours to this place... The wages he earned left him without the option of divorce, child support. If this place *did* close down, his only future would be an independent hardware store, as worker, possibly manager. His life (like so many, many others) was a vicious cycle of working to exist, hand to mouth...

Lastly, I stole a look at Woody, still absorbed in his crosswords... As much as I like this guy, his aspiration in this life was to keep a roof over his head, and get high in front of the T.V. Again, provided this place stayed in business, he would be here for the next twenty years, cutting lumber, hoping he didn't lose a few fingers along the way...

I quietly looked about, following my assessment... Woody, from lumber; swallowed up by his crosswords, burning up what few remaining brain cells he possessed... Brian–the guy I had pegged for a slightly older, cool breeze; now revealed as an overloaded, terrified, well-concealed mess... And Carolyn–sadly, Carolyn–whose next fifteen years were spoken for... Carolyn, who would be thirty-five, before her kid would have a life of her own (hopefully). Carolyn, whose resentment and bitterness (and regret, possibly regret), at being a young mother; ending up like so many women, who would have chosen otherwise, rather than sacrifice their own lives; working menial jobs, forsaking an education...

The hum of the sickly overhead fluorescents, the dirty coffee pot, which hadn't been used for years; the smelly refrigerator, told me I was experiencing one last look at this place, as well as well as these people... People who I was more fortunate than in terms of optimism, and enthusiasm... People I would maybe think about, in times to come... In a weird way, people I had loved...

I deliberately took one minute of silence... mmmm.

"Well..." I said, to no one in particular. "Back to basics..." With that, I pushed away from the table, and left the break room.

Betty was waiting on a customer, lavishing him with her expertise of paint, acrylics... The customer was a man, towering over her less than five-and-a-half-foot frame... He seemed enthralled.

I had a feeling I was taking one last look at her, as well... This basically pleasant woman–the fondness for who has been worn thin, by familiarity, repetition–and secretly wished her the best... She had been here close to ten years–first Builder's World, and now Builder's Mart.

When the customer left, she regarded me the way she always did upon my return from break.

I looked straight at her. "Betty," I said, firmly, throwing positive energies her way. "Once in a lifetime..."

She looked at me intently, for a moment, and only she could see if she understood.

"Once in a lifetime," she repeated, and I concluded she understood–she was far too tough a cookie to not have...

My uneventful half-hour for lunch, the remainder of the day flew by, almost dreamlike, the way the latter half of some days do...

As soon as I walked out into the blinding, beautiful sunlight, the gruesome sense of that place disappeared forever behind me... I got into my car, which was long since warm, smelled of sunlight...

Tomorrow is school; I won't see this place for three days... Hopefully, by the end of next school year, I won't see this place, again...

I drove off...

THE END

DUSK

By Ralph Freda

'It's just like going a bit farther out...'

This was the rationalization Janice Jankowski used to herself, pertaining to how she would handle her homeless friend... Janice Jankowski was a resident of Newport Beach (more specifically, a semi-private island of Newport Beach), fifty-six years of age, the mother of two grown children (one in college, one off 'finding himself'), and three years widowed from a wealthy husband. He passed away at an age far too young, in his favorite chair, one evening after they returned from their favorite restaurant - in fact they had each just finished their favorite meal, brought to them by their favorite server.

The 8:00 p.m. summer sun was setting - a golden California sunset cast a magnificent, inimitable light throughout the eighth floor of their Lido Island condo...and Ron had a massive heart attack while Janice was peeing in the next room.

Dead, almost instantly.

His insurance and assets left her more than three million dollars...and very much alone. Their daughter was grown, and already in college. Their son, a fusion of hippy and God-knew-what, and living on his own; so it was up to Janice to get her act together, and make a life for herself.

She had lived all her life in Newport Beach, though not Lido Island - her father was a self-made millionaire, and though she had been privileged, she was hardly spoiled. She grew up knowing everybody in Newport Beach, socializing. with everyone; every social circle.

So, when she met Ron, he was young and promising - beginning to make money - and in the end became a multi-millionaire in real estate banking. They had two beautiful, healthy children, never left Newport Beach, and for the most part had a fairy tale life.

But then Ron died suddenly, and she was alone to sort out her days.

Money wasn't a problem - the condo was paid for. Ron had left her an estate valued at over three million, and she had attorneys and accountants who were also lifelong friends to guide her. It was the tedium - there was only so much boutique shopping you could do, so many lunches with your friends, sad to say, but so many conversations with your own daughter, up at Berkeley.

'It's just like going a bit farther out...', was a line her father would use to coach her, when he taught her to swim. Although they lived five minutes from the Pacific, the roar of the ocean was too mighty for a small girl to learn to swim - no, they had a grand swimming pool of their own, and he had taught her there.

Janice would start in the shallow end, and work her way, fearfully, to the deep. Her father would stride alongside, upon the concrete edge of the pool, ready to dive in at a moment's notice. She would doggie-paddle, furiously pumping, focused on the deep end, but all the while knowing she was in her father's peripheral vision.

Farther and farther out, during the course of summer, he had taught her to swim.

2.

Janice first became aware of the homeless man whilst upon her daily routine; an easy-breezy Newport Beach autumn day - not a cloud in the sky; nor, for most of its residents, a care in the world. She tooled about in her white, four-door Mercedes R-class (2012, as Ron had left her the latest model, before departing); first to Fashion Island (an outdoor shopping mall, which happened to be the most high-end in the country), then to meet friends for lunch, then to Trader Joe's to pick up a small roast, as it was Janice's habit to pick that evening's dinner up the same day.

Then on to the post office; then home to fix dinner.

The homeless man was plopped dead-center upon the lawn, in front of the Newport Beach Post Office - it was a smaller, sister branch, so there was far less traffic to contend with, mostly for people who lived in a private community, a block away. It was a small, one-level red brick building, obscured, for the most part, by well-maintained foliage, and landscaping. As much as Janice went out of her way to come here, she resided upon luxurious Lido Island (semi-private, thank you very much), this is where she chose to receive her mail.

Needless to say, she was shocked at the contrasting sight of a homeless man, sitting Indian-style upon a blanket, in front of her beloved post office. He was fairly young (couldn't had been more than thirty- five years of age). Caucasian. Short brown hair. She couldn't tell from a distance, but if she had to guess, other than young, Janice Jankowski would eve n have said he was handsome.

There is an overwhelming conscious reaction, in modern times, to be underwhelmed by the sight of homeless people, to consciously preclude them, upon sight. Usually, they are one of three circumstances of indigent (static, upon some street corner, surrounded by everything they own; endlessly pushing a shopping cart, piled high with everything they own; or filthy, dirty, holding a begging sign, just off the exit of your local freeway). Probably worse than conscious ignorance of these people, is assuming they are completely harmless, and that they have no violent agenda, or designs whatsoever, upon the people surrounding them.

One forgets that they not only live without societal structure and cohesion, and are willing to do so, but something quite significant has occurred to get them to that point.

Their existence, twenty-four hours a day, three-hundred sixty-five days a year, is quite unimaginable to most of the world.

So, for the second time since spotting him, what weighed slightly upon Janice was the sheer bizarreness at the sight of this young man sitting upon the lawn, obviously displaced, wearing dirty clothing (jeans, t-shirt); dirty bundle of clothes (mostly torn and rag-like) strewn about him, and two water bottles, half filled, with colored liquid.

'No shopping cart, though' she thought to herself; which was odd, because usually when one sees the homeless nowadays, they have such an accumulation of possessions, not willing (or unable, it seemed, to Janice) to part with a one.

Janice sat with the motor of her Mercedes idling for a minute, ambivalent of what to do. It was still post office hours, so employees were present, yet there were only two other cars in the lot. To get into the tiny building, she would have to walk past this man, sitting Indian-style, upon the lawn, four feet outside the door.

She sat in silence, debating, as the excellent motor purred, in the perfect afternoon.

Mustering her courage, and knowing the pork roast she had bought at Trader Joe's, and which was beside her in the Mercedes, for tonight's dinner, would spoil, she grabbed her small purse by Mui Mui, exited the car, locked it via the electronic key, and walked toward the small brick building.

As the building, and needless to say, the indigent man, became closer, a distant feeling of anxiety came over Janice. Her walk from the car to inside the post office was no more than ten yards, but the whole thing was happening in slow motion, her legs seemed suddenly heavier than they usually did, and she was sure she felt her heart rate increase.

It seemed to take forever.

'You're being ridiculous' she admonished herself, reflecting that she couldn't ask to be in a safer, more controlled environment; safer circumstances.

She was determined that when she walked past him, she would not look at him; would not make eye contact, even were he to be looking at her.

Going immediately past him, her eye was helplessly pulled sideways upon him - he was not looking at her. He, in fact, was sitting exactly the way she at first had discovered him - Indian-style, looking ahead, in the distance, as if fixated with some distant memory. There was a surreal vacuum of silence as she passed.

Clutching her expensive Miu Miu, she entered the small post office, only this time, without the relaxed certainty of a Newport Beach resident, without a care in the world. Though it was a perfect, breezy seventy degree autumn day outside, the inside of the small post office was immaculate and air conditioned - Spanish tiles on the floor; two coats of the best satin paint on the walls, where there were boxes.

Today was Saturday, so there was only one worker behind the counter, two patrons at their boxes. Janice made a beeline for her personal box, retrieved the key from her purse, and gathered her mail.

Thinking ahead, she knew she would not quickly sort through today's mail in the Mercedes (as was her usual custom); not with the homeless man out there, like that, so she tucked her bag up under her arm, and quickly went through what had arrived.

Her body exuded a thrush of relief when she realized it was all junk mail.

Replacing her box key back into her purse, Janice turned and headed back out to her car, pausing only to throw the junk mail into the trash can, near the door.

She pushed through the glass double-doors, and focused on her Mercedes, this time the man on her left side, rather than her right. Again, he was silent; again, a surreal vacuum of quiet about him, as she passed.

Janice stopped at the door of her car, and silently cursed herself for not thinking ahead to take her car keys from her purse, and have them ready. She quickly - as quickly as her hands would allow - rummaged through the contents of her purse (top-of-the-line cell phone, five-hundred-dollar wallet, apartment keys), until she came to the Mercedes Benz key ring, hiding at the bottom - it had been Ron's, and he had left it to her along with the car. She electronically unlocked the door, feeling reassured, upon hearing the double 'squelching' noise; opened the door, got in behind the wheel, and immediately locked the car.

3.

Once Janice was behind the wheel for, and in a familiar, safe environment she could control, it took her a good two minutes of silent calm, for her to truly feel secure. Her attention went immediately to her homeless friend, just outside the post office - still Indian-style, still looking off, as if too tired from some impossible mathematical problem. Janice recalled one thing from the fleeting glimpse of him: he was handsome, but in an offbeat way: angular face; high cheeckbones. Janice couldn't make out the color of his eyes, but his short-cropped hair was a dishwater blonde. Even a quick look at him revealed a three-day growth of the same blonde-brown beard on his face.

Finally, she put the ignition key into the ignition, ready to head home, the remainder of the evening planned out in her head - the pork roast in the seat beside her was to go into the oven (as was the sauerkraut, potatoes); she would get on the phone with her daughter, at Berkeley; she would catch up on emails to her friends; she would watch her favorite shows on television.

But this fellow on the lawn -what was his evening to be? Obviously, people have come and gone all day - possibly for days, or longer - and not said or done anything to help him. Janice gripped both hands loosely upon the wheel of her Mercedes, and for the life of her, could not put out of her Christian mind, the thought of thoughtlessly turning her back on this indigent man - who seemingly had nothing - while she went back to a million-dollar condo, on Lido Island.

She opened her Miu Miu, went to the Luis Vuitton wallet, and went past the bills she had there.

'This is your lucky day', she thought to herself, as she never carried cash - even when she bought coffee for herself, she had a Starbucks card, preferring to tip at the end of the month. She went past a five dollar bill, two one dollar bills, and settled upon a twenty. She removed the twenty from her purse, and closed her purse back up, securing it.

She started the Mercedes. Of course, the engine came to life and hummed like a dream. She sat in the car, with the engine idling for a moment, and she realized her homeless man was now looking her way, gazing at her, sitting in the car, and she knew why - by this time, Janice had been in the car for the better part of five minutes.

He probably thought *she* was in need of help.

The twenty dollar bill was pinched between her right thumb and forefinger; she was just about to put the car into drive, and approach him, to roll the window down, and Janice felt her nerve diminish.

It was then a thought-from the past occurred to her.

'It's just like going a bit farther out...'

It was what her father used to tell her when she was a little girl - she in their pool, paddling for her very life; him walking alongside her, swearing he would never leave...that she could not fail.

'There's nothing to be afraid of Janice', she reassured herself. It's broad daylight outside; there's still a handful of people in the post office. 'Besides', she concluded. 'you're in a running vehicle. If there's trouble, just drive away.'

So, with that in mind, along with what her father would tell her, poolside when she was a child, she slowly drove up where this indigent stranger was sitting Indian-style upon the lawn in Newport Beach and rolled the car slowly to a stop, five or so feet away. The whole time she did, this, she never took her eyes from him, and as he rolled to a halt, Janice noticed he had turned his head to look at her through the open car window, with almost a kind of telepathy. Also, she saw now, what she hadn't before noticed - his eyes were the coldest blue. An icy blue. They didn't stare; yet they looked out ahead of him; as he was a young man, able bodied; who sat all day, with too much time, and without direction and purpose.

"Sir!" Janice spoke quickly, mustering her voice; getting it out, and over with. "Sir...let me give you something..." She put the Mercedes in 'park', crossed her right hand with the twenty in it over the steering wheel, and held it tentatively out the open window - quite frankly ready to either blare the horn, throw the car into 'drive' and peel out, or both, if necessary.

There was what seemed an eternity of silence, as the man simply seemed to continue to sit, silently, looking back at Janice. Overwhelmingly, when money is offered to people in such circumstances, they are ready for such opportunities, they physically spring up at the instant they see the currency afforded them - this one continued to sit Indian-style, as if contemplating Janice; her words; what she attempting do for him.

Again, the bizarre thought of telepathy occurred to Janice, and she was just about to renege, for feeling a fool, when suddenly, yet at the same time, seemingly, slowly, the youngish man started getting to his feet.

Surely - as we know this moment was not about to go backward in time - the man got to his feet (somewhat, Janice observed, more steadily than she would have expected); in fact, looking slightly to the left and right, walked rather confidently and briskly toward her Mercedes, closing the ten-foot gap between them.

He came up to the car door, but not immediately- eighteen inches away, and Janice clearly saw for the first time what she had seen when she had earlier passed, on the way into the post office: he couldn't have been more than his middle thirties, as far.as age was concerned. His hair was a walnut brown; close-cropped, as if he has done it himself. Ruggedly handsome, with a thin face, and high cheek bones. A three-day, walnut-colored beard upon his face.

But what struck Janice - almost paralyzingly so - were his icy blue eyes.

The whole time he came up to the car - from the moment he got up from the lawn - his eyes fixed upon her, and didn't move. They looked slightly to the left, slightly to the right (as if for oncoming traffic, which in itself was odd, as this was the parking lot of a tiny post office), and then fixed themselves straight upon Janice; looking her right in the eye, until he stood, in silence, eighteen inches away.

He simply stood in abject silence, as if an actor who absolutely refused to help a fellow actress who had suddenly 'gone up' on her lines.

It was all she could do, but look helplessly back, through the half-rolled down window.

Somehow, her words of a minute prior came to her.

"Sir," Janice Jankowski said, suddenly aware of how solitary her voice sounded. "Let me give you something." She still clutched the twenty in her right hand. The Mercedes was still running, and although she has no intention of either turning off the engine, or further rolling down the window, she mustered her confidence enough to hand the twenty through the half rolled-down window.

Wordlessly, and somehow gracefully, the man reached silently up, and took the twenty-dollar bill from Janice Jankowski's right hand. Not a word of 'thanks', nor even acknowledgment; never even regarding the denomination of the bill - simply brought his arm slowly back down to his side, turned slowly around, and went to sit back down, Indian-style, upon his spot.

Janice watched all this, with the Mercedes motor running - she was distantly baffled by such oddish behavior, especially the completely silence in which the entire transaction took occurred.

Finally, the car's running motor snapped her out of her daze. She rolled the window up all the way, took one final look at the indigent man, sitting Indian-style, in front of the post office, recalled her pork roast on the front seat, getting warmer with every passing moment, and drove home.

4.

Later that night, Janice lie in bed, turning over in her mind the most unusual event, of earlier that day. The small pork roast had been cooked, eaten, and put away. The small portion of asparagus, and even smaller portion of new potatoes; the remainders of which also dutifully put away.

Following dinner, she made her nightly, routine phone calls to her friends - caught up on whatever innocuous gossip was around (most of which she could live without; as anyone knew at her age, nothing juicy happened for anyone, anyway).

Janice was careful not to bring up - to anyone - her encounter with the indigent man outside the post office, *especially* - dear God, *especially* - her daughter, up in college at Berkeley, who would have at a moment's notice jumped in her car, driven down to Newport Beach, and had her mother committed to psychiatric institution, for even *daring* to do such a thing.

But one thing bothered Janice, as she lie in bed - ten stories up, on an exclusive island, in Newport Beach - a world away, yet not so very long ago from the man of earlier that day, and his world. What her mind kept focusing on were his eyes - his blue, blue eyes. Not icy blue; but in no way warm, or inviting. They were neither accusing, nor imploring, and when she had given him the money (or wasn't it that he had expected it?), his eyes were neither grateful, nor happy.

Where was he now? Was he still even there - sleeping outside somewhere, near the post office? Is that what these people did?

It wasn't until two hours later, just as Janice was drifting off to sleep, that she bolted wide awake with the realization of what it was that was bothering her - it was the telepathic surety that right at that (this) very moment - as she lay in bed - he also was not only wide awake, but thinking of her, concentrating on her, focused on her.

Calling her back...

Waiting for her...

Janice, upon, realizing this, understanding this, and somehow seeing in her mind's eye the indigent man; somewhere, out there, calling to her - felt her entire body finally relax; and she submitted down into the final throes of sleep and dreams.

5.

The following afternoon was Sunday, Janice and her friend, Sommer, sat having their luncheon, within Bloomingdale's cafe - Naughty Near Park Ave. - within Fashion Island. About them, thousands (far overwhelmingly female) of wealthy clientele bustled determinately throughout the enormous Newport Beach mecca.

Janice picked at her House Chopped Salad, more throwing it to one side of the larger than necessary glass bowl than the other. Her friend, Sommer, having noticed Janice's taciturn manner through lunch, said, "If we have desert, are you going to play with *that to*?!"

To which Janice caught herself, set the fork down calmly into the bowl, and replied, "I'm sorry, Sommer." She tried smiling. "I guess I've something on my mind."

Sommer took a pause. "Tell me."

Janice regarded her friend.

Sommer DiCardo was herself German/Spanish, married to a Newport Beach Italian-American multi- millionaire. She was draped, head to toe, in ostentatious jewelry and clothing; all of it more than some physicians earn in a year. Janice Jankowski could not-would not relate her story of yesterday's events to her.

"It's nothing." She said, finally.

"*Jan..*", Sommer emphasized, leaning forward, over her Cobb Salad. "*You* are never preoccupied about *anything... tell me...*" Then as Janice looked into her friend's imploring face, and as the scent of her perfume (the *best*, of course) somehow came across the table, it occurred to her that she really had no one in the world with whom to talk - she had this extraordinary experience yesterday, and not a soul in the world with whom she could share. Her husband was dead. Her daughter wouldn't understand. Her son... who saw him?

Janice looked sullenly down at her place at the table, considered the helpful words of her friend; suddenly identified very much like the man she met·the day before - the man without a soul in the world.

"Sommer, you wouldn't believe it." She finally gushed, going on for five minutes, ending with, "...and now I find this man consumes my every waking thought - like some stray animal that's somehow my responsibility, and that I'm wronging."

Sommer, who had listened in silence to her friend speak, sat silently, further still.

Their lunch entrees sat upon the table between them, while customers (ladies, for the most part) went about the restaurant, and about their day.

The silence was definite.

"Jan", Sommer said, finally. "I'm aghast at what you've told me."

Janice looked back at her, trying to be even - she more or less knew how she had sounded.

Sommer went on, "Jan, honey, don't you know - these people are *dangerous*?! Most of them are *mentally ill*, for God's sake?! (here Sommer made a 'yukko' noise to exclaim her disgust).

"I don't know if he actually *lives* there," Janice said weakly.

"Jan, I won't hear another word of this drivel! Ron would be spinning in his grave, if he knew!" Sommer mentioning Ron went through Janice like lightning, and it brought her back closer to reality.

Their server passed, Sommer asked for their check, and they got ready to leave.

"I can't imagine what your *kids* would say about this, Jan." Of course, this was another bolt of lightning going through her; another example of how bizarrely detached the whole situation was from the norm.

Forget, forget, forget the idea of sharing the idea Janice had of perhaps putting together a forty dollar goodie-basket for the gentleman...this was out. Sommer would have her committed; call her daughter up at Berkeley.

No, her German Spanish millionaire friend was a million happy miles away from the life this poor indigent man lived, and sadly, Janice thought, perhaps even from myself, as well.

"You know" Sommer concluded, as they prepared to leave that afternoon. "I'm not even sure I want you using that Post Office so long as he's around."

"Sommer," Janice said weakly. "I'lll be fine."

"Well...okay. You carry your cell with you at all times, right?!"

"Right."

SO, after saying 'goodbyes', and pecks upon cheeks, the two friends parted ways, in the perfect autumn day of the California sun.

6.

Of course, the first thing Janice did following her luncheon with Sommer was make a bee-line for Trader Joe's - this was not to say this was unusual for her daily routine (she picked up her nightly dinner *every* day); this time she went shopping for two.

The one thing her luncheon with Sommer had convinced her of, she was very out of touch with people's suffering. She had been brought up in luxury, but she had been brought up Catholic; raised in a first-generation Polish immigrant home, where the people there were grateful for what they had; didn't forget to give back to people, when they could.

'Okay...The forty-dollar gift basket is *out*,' she thought to herself. "Maybe just a couple of sandwiches.'

Janice arrived at Trader Joe's, carefully parked the Mercedes, and went in. The usual melee of Newport Beach housewives, younger and older, went about, baskets on their arms - it was a Heaven of lower-end gourmet items. Looking about, this only reinforced Janice's thoughts and feelings of how obligated she was toward her homeless friend.

Going to the cooler that held fish, she chose a salmon filet for dinner.

Now something for her friend...

She went to the cooler that held ready-made sandwiches and breakfast burritos - anything frozen was out, as he didn't have access to a microwave. There were tuna salad sandwiches on rye; turkey, bacon, lettuce, and tomato on wheat. Janice thought they ALL looked good to someone starving, and living outside a Post Office.

Finally, Janice settled on two tuna wraps - they were large - three inches around, made with pita bread, and garnished with lettuce.

She placed the wraps in her basket next to her salmon, and made for the checkout counter. Once there, she saw small boxes of chocolate-covered coffee beans, and thought they'd be a nice touch with the sandwiches.

"Will that be all?" the checkout girl asked.

"Yes," Janice said, "thank you." And paid for her items, and left.

Her luncheon with Sommer had began later than usual, and so it had ended later than usual - by the time she had left Fashion Island for Trader Joe's, it was almost four in the afternoon. Now, having shopped for her dinner, and the wraps for her homeless friend, it was going on five.

The problem was it was getting dark.

Driving to the Post Office, she ran over again and again in her mind exactly how she was going to handle confronting this person - she had never done something such as this before. What if Sommer was right? What *if* he was dangerous? Psychotic. Janice recalled the last time she called him over to the car; recalled how brave she had been.

Janice remembered the words of her father: 'It's just like going a bit farther out...'

Those words, spoken to her, when she was a girl learning to swim, came back to her now. All those decades ago, her strong, loving father, walking the edge of the pool, had made sure she would make it to the deep end; and she had…eventually.

It was a matter of going a bit farther out.

Surely enough, Janice arrived at the Post Office - only now a glance at the Mercedes clock said almost five-thirty. It was autumn, and the although it was by now dusk, the sky held a beautiful sun that was setting far in the west. Thin clouds hung, obscuring what would otherwise have been a perfect sunset.

Although Janice had been psyching herself up for this, as the Post Office came into view, she found herself wishing her homeless friend would not be in residence.

This, of course, was not the case - as soon as Janice pulled the Mercedes into the parking lot of the small Post Office, her eyes made out (barely) the pyramid-shape of her homeless friend sitting Indian-style in his usual spot.

Janice's hands tensed upon the wheel - it was dark now; besides which, everyone else had long since gone home for the day. Also, it was unlikely, any patrons would happen by. Indeed, the Post Office took on a completely different light from the way she knew it to be - it was now dark and eerie, and this person sat like a solitary, sinister proprietor.

'I'll just hand him the sandwiches, and be gone,' she thought to herself. 'Go straight home, cook dinner, and forget I ever did this.'

She parked the car in a space in the small lot, not far from where he sat, and turned off the motor. Her windows were still rolled up, and sneaking a peak, she saw he had not moved, or even seemed at all to notice her presence.

Her mind, being rushed by the unknown circumstances of her situation - the fact that this man was a stranger, the lateness of the hour, the fact no one was around - caused her to clutch apprehensively the paper bag from Trader Joe's, as to not lose her nerve. She reached past her salmon filet, and brought out the tuna wraps, along with the small box of chocolate covered espresso beans.

She placed the keys to the Mercedes in.her purse, leaving both alongside her groceries, as she was returning immediately back to the car. Then, gathering the foodstuffs within the crook of her right arm, and bracing her left hand on the handle of the car, Janice realized she had no spit in her mouth, whatsoever.

She exited the car, and began walking (if you would call it that) toward the now dimly-lit pyramid shape of him, just a few yards ahead. As her legs trembled beneath her, Janice recalled how she had only seen this man up close but once, and never heard the sound of his voice

- he had wordlessly taken the money she had earlier offered.

The gap between them was closing, closing, and Janice was being overwhelmed simultaneously by three elements: the early darkness of Autumn (which she could kick herself for allowing to happen in the first place), the absolute stillness with which this man sat in the encroaching darkness (though Janice saw he had by now taken notice of her, and was watching as she approached), and the unnatural, almost supernatural vacuum of silence that enveloped her, as she approached this man.

Janice didn't know what she was doing - way out of her element, she had the wild desire to fling the tuna wrap and chocolate-covered espresso beans at him, turn, and run. It was then she heard the voice of her father; the words he would use to encourage her: 'It's just like going a bit farther out!', and believe it or not, these words brought her the few final steps up to him.

Finally, face to face (Janice standing with a small armful of food; the man sitting Indian-style), they regarded each other in semi-darkness, and in silence.

"Good evening," Janice mustered, feeling absurd, but trying to be cheery. "I hope you won't take offense to this - I noticed you here again, tonight, so I thought you might enjoy a wonderful sandwich and some chocolate."

Janice held out the two items to him in the dim light, so that he may see them, but she also used the opportunity to register a closer, better look at him. Just as she remembered, he was youngish, fairly rugged-looking, with a thin face and angular, high cheekbones. What she couldn't see in the dimness, however, were the particular staring, icy-blue eyes of his - the eyes she couldn't look away from the day earlier, and perhaps the eyes she had expected again on seeing, now.

She watched as he regarded her in silence - her simply standing there, still holding out the food - then, she had the anticipatory feeling he would respond. And he silently, looking up at her, he reached up with both hands, and took with either hand, the tuna wrap, and the espresso beans.

Janice was surprised further still when he placed the food items at either side of him, brought his leg out from under himself, and stood slowly upon his feet. Finally, at eye-level to her, he spoke for the first time. "Thank you," he said.

His voice was young, confident, and healthy, rather surprising Janice and catching her off-guard at the same time. She countered it by saying "I hope I haven't embarrassed or offended you."

"Oh, no ma'am," the man was quick to reply. "You'd be surprised how very *few* of the people who come through here actually offer to help. I can't thank you *enough*."

"I'm not surprised," she said. "The people here have nothing but money, yet they're as greedy as sin." After a moment, Janice asked, "May I ask, what is your name?"

There was the most noticeable pause - palpable - and just as it occurred to Janice that it was getting very dark out, and this man was a stranger, he extinguished the moment by speaking. "John. My name is John."

Janice smiled. "How do you do, John? I'm Janice."

John seemed to assimilate to name of his new friend for a moment, and then smiled and said, "Janice. How do you do, Janice?" John looked down at the food at either side of his feet, and an awkward moment of silence rose up in the coming darkness. Janice was about to say her 'goodbye' when John brought his head up. "Would you like to see where I live?"

"I'm sorry," was all she could manage.

"Where I live," he continued explaining. "My things - I keep them stashed around yonder; back of the Post Office."

This caught Janice totally off guard - she had no idea how to respond. On one hand, this man was a total stranger, on the other, he seemed harmless enough, compounded with the fact he didn't have a friend in the world.

"Oh, I don't know, John. I must be getting along. Plus, it's getting awfully dark out."

Even in the very low light, she could make out a broad smile across his thin, rugged, handsome face. "It'll be *okay*," he said. "Just a minute. You're the only person who has been kind to me since I've been here. Please."

Something coming over Janice - a calm she couldn't explain (perhaps her father's words of, 'It's just like going a bit farther out' - made her trepidation evaporate. She found herself saying, "Alright, John."

9

"Good," John said, warmly, barely more than a shadow. "I'm glad. My stuff is around this way. Follow me."

He started walking around the small red brick building, Janice in tow. By design, the building was small, but the landscaping was such that six-foot hedges were meticulously put in all around the perimeter of the small Post Office. By now, the sun was almost gone, and the two of them looked as though ghosts.

Just around the first corner, John stepped back and, more or less indicated, to Janice with his left arm his small camp/home.

Janice, following, came hesitantly around the corner- not sure what she would find. Following the direction of where John had indicated, peering off into the impossible darkness, she strained to see what was indeed a small gathering of belongings. Everything was very vague in the dimness; impossible to make out.

She looked at him. "It's very hard for me to see in this light. May I?"

"Oh!" John said, suddenly smiling, though you couldn't tell in the darkness. "I wish you would!"

At this, Janice took the necessary steps forward to inspect his home - what she didn't see was John slowly, quietly reached around with his right arm, lifted up his shirt, and retrieved a box-cutter he had stashed in the small of his back, in his jeans.

"How long have you lived here?" Janice asked aloud, yet almost to herself- she was astonished at the degradation.

"Not long," John replied in an even voice. "I move around quite a bit. Besides, the people around here aren't really that keen on people like me, so..."

Janice turned to look at this poor man - she could barely begin to understand a human being dispossessed by other human beings. John took two slow steps toward her, aware of her sympathy, and closing the gap between them.

"Don't feel bad" he said. "I have plenty of places to go; lots of good people like you."

Janice took a moment to genuinely struggle for the right words. "It's just that I wish I could do more."

As she spoke, John opened the box-cutter three clicks, to the length he desired.

There was a thick silence between them; thick as the dusk.

After a long moment, John spoke. "I figure this is dark enough."

Janice, who hadn't quite heard or understood, was just about to ask, "Dark enough for what?" when if by some telepathy, John answered aloud "For anyone to see." And with that, with all his might, brought his right arm round, box-cutter in hand, and sliced Janice cleanly across her throat, severing in one stroke her jugular vein, and windpipe.

10

At first, Janice was only aware physically that he had done something to her; had somehow swiped her, seemingly across the neck - it was so dark, by now, she couldn't really see, and there wasn't an immediate pain; more of an acute pinch across the breadth of her throat.

She immediately looked at John in bewilderment - about to speak; ask 'what,' and 'why' - and then the pain came; searing hot, across the breadth of her throat, where the pinch had been. Janice brought her hands up to her neck, as if to help. As if to investigate what John had done. By tilting her head back ever so, she separated the wound, and found that her hands were covering a fatal gash, that was just beginning to lose massive amounts of blood.

John merely took a silent step back, box-cutter at his side.

Janice's bewilderment increased, and as her mind fumbled for something to say, blood was by now backed-up into her mouth, which made her unable to speak.

"The world is an awesome place" John said to her, distinctly and slowly in the darkness. "It goes by real slow."

Janice dropped to her knees. She had heard his words, but was unable to comprehend them. By now she was losing consciousness from blood loss, and would soon be dead. She fell onto her back, upon the lawn, blood weakly pumping from the fatal wound.

As Janice Jankowski lay dying behind the small Post Office, the final thoughts that went through her bewildered mind were of her life, her children, and the salmon filet from Trader Joe's upon the front seat of the Mercedes, which surely be going bad by now.

11.

When John (that never really was his name, anyway), looked at Janice and saw she was dead - or at least still enough, silent enough to be - walked several feet to his pile of belongings, picked up a large, dirty sweatshirt, and covered her face. By now it was so dark one could barely make out the shape of her body, which they wouldn't discover until the next day; possibly days later than that.

She had died hardly without a sound.

Dropping the box-cutter, he walked silently across the small parking lot to the Mercedes. Of course, the door was unlocked, and when he got behind the wheel, discovered the keys still in the ignition, as Janice had left them. He discovered also the salmon filet, which he had no use for, but was more interested in the contents of Janice's purse - mostly credit cards, less than twenty dollars in cash.

The new owner of the slightly-used Mercedes started the car. He had his options - North on highway, 101, or east to Las Vegas? It would be a full day until the landscapers discovered the body, identified it, and went looking for the car. If he went toward Nevada starting now, he could easily make the state line.

'Who knows' he thought to himself. 'Perhaps a bit further out...'

SATURDAYS

By Ralph Freda

Chicken Fantastic was really a subsidiary of its parent company–Chicken Delicious – which was headquartered all the way across the country, in California (we were now in Illinois)... Chicken Fantastic was the brainchild of three Harvard school graduates, whose wealthy parents backed their brilliant idea, that *anything* marketed well enough, would sell...

Planted firmly in suburbia, it was a favorite of bachelors, and entire families, alike – the bachelors did the drive through, after work (occasionally a solitary, lonely bachelor would do dine-in, unable to spend another lonely night, eating before the T.V.); the families (with more working mothers these days) would do drive through.

Eddie had been the proud 'associate' of the Chicken Fantastic family for exactly six months – coming aboard in December, it was now May, and the snow that had been piled up to the drive-thru window was long gone; the fierce, freezing winds that blew the doors of the restaurant shut, as soon as they were opened, now were gentle warm waves; the stomping of galoshes was replaced, mostly by sneakers...

If you were young, it was a great place to work; simultaneously, notoriously, also the worst... The greatest aspect, that there was hardly any business – a small independent name wasn't a raving favorite with the people. Thirty-minute, delivered pizzas, bigger-name, nationally-established fried chicken places, and higher-end burgers were favorites. The worst aspect – the really shitty part of the job – was shoving your hands (albeit, gloved) into buckets of chicken livers, awaiting the breading able, constantly washing your hands, for fear of salmonella... And the smell of chicken – *augghhh*, you *reeked* of chicken – lasted upon your person for days

9:30 a.m. sharp, Eddie came in for his Saturday shift. Most kids got there five or ten minutes early, and sat in their cars, smoking one last cigarette (or joint, as the case sometimes was), before coming in at the very last minute. Eddie was already uniformed – a white shirt,

purchased by him (taken out of his first check), and dark brown,
heavier trousers (also taken from his first check). Chicken Fantastic
supplied the name tag, paper hats, and of course, the plastic gloves
needed to reach for un-breaded chicken livers, chicken parts...

As soon as he opened the rear door of the place (unlocked by
Curtis, the manager), a warm, heavily pressurized gust of air washed
over him; warm, and thick with the odor of tens of thousands of orders
of fried chicken prepared over the years... Anyone who's ever worked
fast food knows the particular stink of *wherever* you work, never comes
out... Eddie's mother lovingly, dutifully washed his uniform, but to no
avail – the pants and shirt reeked unbelievably (though he no longer
noticed it, of course) when he got home, and following their being
washed, it was still strong, if held up to the face...

Cha-*chunk* went the time clock – although the mechanism was
digital – letting you know it had read and acknowledged the time card.
Eddie placed his card back in the rack, looking for Sharon's name...
Her car was there, second from the top (his was three below hers). The
sight of her name always gave him a psychic jolt; an impression of her,
that went through his body and mind.

Eddie could've spent the entire day imagining Sharon's presence
alongside him, but he heard the rustlings of Curtis, in the adjacent
kitchen... Grabbing the first available apron, he tied it as he walked
around the corner, into the kitchen. The very first Chicken Fantastic
duty, upon arriving, was to prepare whatever 'side' food they would
need, throughout the day – their 'sides' were basically deep fried
chicken livers, Fantastic Fries (made to order), and mashed potatoes
(instant, of course)...

Curtis was in the kitchen, probably there since 8:00 – now he
was beside the stainless steel vat, pouring into it a fifty pound bag of
instant mashed potatoes, as the tap ran with hot water... Curtis' large
belly hung out, though still covered dutifully by his 3x-sized, over
starched, over bleached white work shirt. Curtis was his manager, and

though he seemed lazy, he really wasn't; he was never afraid to roll up his sleeves, and get in there... He was a twenty-seven year old, long haired (he kept it as long as Chicken Fantastic would allow; though he got away with longer), grossly overweight, high school dropout (though he *did* have a G.E.D.); he was also the manager of Chicken Fantastic.

Curtis swung his greasy blonde locks around, looked at Eddie.

"Hey, Deysyk," he said.

"Hey, Curtis," Eddie replied, and went to the long, stainless steel sink to wash his hands. Staring directly into the yellowed 'lave los manos' sign, he washed his hands... Snatching a pair of disposable plastic gloves, he noticed Curtis wasn't wearing any gloves at all – in fact, it wasn't likely Curtis 'lave-ed his manos', before taking to the mashed potatoes...

Lazy, Curtis wasn't; unsanitary, he was...

"D'ju go to Karen Belsante's party last night?!", still pouring instant mashed in to vat. Though Curtis was twenty seven, he put his freshman-year education to good use, still showing up at high school parties.

"Nah," Eddie drawled out, trying to sound cool, trying to look anything but stuck for an answer, which he was.

"It was a fuckin' rager!" Curtis exclaimed, and dropping the empty fifty pound bag to the floor; added an afterthought. "Fuckin', everybody was there!"

Curtis picked up the large wooden paddle from behind the vat, and started stirring the day's ration of Fantastic Mashed... The awkward silence that followed his comment was not uncommon, about Eddie... He was a quiet, solitary boy, and never really knowing what to say following such remarks, remained silent... It was a noticeable, awkward thing, and though he was aware of it, chose silence, rather than to sound stupid...

Eddie's Dysyk's story was a heartbreaking one, repeated a

million times – with both boys and girls – across the country, and across the world... He was an only child, raised by a single parent... His father seemed to have departed abruptly when he was nine (he was now sixteen); his mother, who had worked anyway, had kept the house, and there they lived together.

The troubling thing is that Eddie's mom seemed to have slowly degenerated since the departure of his father, just over six years ago... It was never really clear, the reason for the divorce – they never discussed it with him. At first it was thick, awkward silences at the dinner table, or during a family outing... There were late-night, muffled arguments, throughout the house. Eddie stayed in his room, strained to hear of what their topic of argument pertained, but to no avail...

Then, of course, the day his mom and dad sat him down, in the dining room... The air was so heavy with sadness and remorse, it was as one of them was about to announce the other was dead; had perished in some horrible automobile accident...

"Your Father and I have been doing a lot of talking...," it began. "It has nothing to do with you. We love you more than anything..." it had ended, more than an hour later... They had spoken to him in tandem, one of them jumping in when other would flail; and even at the age of ten, Eddie understood their monumental love for him, and the difficulty and awkwardness of this sit-down...

So dad left, and his absence was more than noticed... In fact, as time went on, days stretching into months, months into years, Eddie was aware of something that transcended awkward and became unnatural, with just the presence of one parent... Almost as though you were seeing them naked...

The impact upon his mother was huge. Less and less, she would leave the house – and this was over a period of years, mind you – going about, finally, in a dark brown bathrobe, leaving only to go to the bank, or the grocery store; rarely coming away from the television in her room.

It wasn't simply the loss of interest, the melancholy that was discouraging... his mother had begun to cling to him in a way that was uncomfortable... distantly unnatural... Nothing incestuous – remotely so – yet Eddie was the only male in her life, and she gravitated uncomfortably close...

At precisely 10:00 a.m. (not one minute earlier, or later than expected) the back door opened, to the loud vacuum of de-pressurization of air... Bathed in sunlight for a moment, before entering the greasy tomb of Chicken Fantastic, walked Sharon Komperda... Her five foot-four inch frame wore black cotton stretch pants, white sneakers, and the same mandatory white shirt Eddie and Curtis were required to wear.

Sharon Komperda was the most popular girl in the whole high school. Merely a sophomore, every girl wanted to be her, every guy wanted to fuck her... She went about with an aloof cool; compliments of, "you're so pretty, Sharon!" from the girls, and, "hey, sexy!" from the guys, rolled off her like raindrops, as she walked down the halls, between classes; but what made her genuinely sexy is that she genuinely couldn't care less... She wasn't traditionally beautiful, but she *was* pretty – German/Polish, an Ivory complexion with a sprinkling of freckles across her face. Blue/green eyes, and baby-fine, blonde hair, that she kept shoulder length, and loosely-curled... Her body was feline, and semi-muscular – when she sat in chairs, she curled up in them...

Sharon Komperda's greatest aspect, and half her strength, was her voice... It was distinctive; 'girly' as 'girly' can be. The closest you could come to describing it, would be the 'dumb molls' of the gangster movies of then 30's and 40's, but Sharon Komperda was anything but dumb – she was in academic-level studies, and when she spoke, was quite on top of what she had to say.

She was also a 'stoner', and ran with the pot smoking crowd.

She walked her feline walk over to where the aprons were hung. Eddie watched her, and noticed that when she flipped up the back up her baby-fine hair to accommodate the apron, she seemed immaculate of everything around her... She glowed, somehow... Tying the apron behind her, as she walked toward the steel sink, she shot Eddie, and then Curtis, a telepathic, half-resentful, purr of 'hello'. The three of them – as with so many workers, especially in morning hours – come to develop their own telepathy.

Sharon approached the steel sink, and opened the tap with her elbow, the way only girls can. When she finally did look up, at whoever was around to meet her gaze, it happened to be Eddie. She spoke over the loud spatter of water hitting the basin.

"Hi:.!" in this 'dumb as a brick voice', but was anything but. This beautiful girl- who you actually swear was both an angel and a sexpot was tough-as-nails, smoked pot, maintained academic-level studies, fist-fought, and had been sexually active since the age of fourteen, with her boyfriend and lover of eight months younger than she...

"Hey, Sharon," Eddie said casually, trying to sound cool.

Sharon just regarded him for moment; finished washing her hands – it was too early in the morning (on a Saturday, no less) for insincere cordiality.

By now Curtis was done with the instant mashed potatoes, and broke in with his gruff voice. "Okay, you guys! You know the drill..! Sharon, Eddie and me did livers and gizzards. You got legs, breasts, and, thighs..."

The whole time Curtis addressed her, she looked at him with a feline contempt. It wasn't a contempt for the work, which was bad enough, so much as contempt for this fat, slovenly, manager, who put no effort of regard, or politeness, when addressing a girl. Eddie watched her, mesmerized; almost thought he heard Sharon hiss, as she stood there, listening to Curtis.

The spell was broken when he turned to Eddie. "Eddie, you got the Juicer." Then, somehow, he shot a look at both of them simultaneously. "Let's go! Chop-chop!"

At that, Eddie was into gear and started to move; but Sharon was frozen in defiance. By now she has finished washing her hands, but Curtis' command of 'chop-chop' didn't set well with her, and the drumming of the running water hitting the steel basin uncomfortably loud... She locked her gaze with Curtis, and Curtis stared back... He could get away with 'chop-chop' at Friday or Saturday night kegger parties, when everyone was drunk, or high, and feeling good; but during the merciless sobriety of Saturday mornings, that was a 'no-no'.

"What, Komperda?!" He said, trying to sound incredulous, but knowing he was going to lose. Sharon only returned his stare, saying nothing. Eddie watched for a moment, and understood that this girl was more than fire – she was the meaning of life, itself... After a moment of locking eyes, and what seemed an eternity of spattering of the running of water (Sharon had not yet turned off the tap) Curtis capitulated. "Come on, just get to work..."

The half-pleading worked with her, and she reluctantly started to move, beginning by saving Chicken Fantastic an enormous water bill, and then drying her hands.

Eddie got busy dusting the chicken parts (by now they had forty-five minutes until they opened their doors), while Sharon counted out the money for the registers, which was usually her job... Soon enough, as and was with most Saturdays, Cutis and Sharon got into the back and forth rhythm of the goings on of the previous Friday night: who had gotten outrageously drunk, or high, or both; who had approached who, while being in such a state, fraught with heartbreak, claiming they couldn't go on; who had fist fought, and where; various drag races (Curtis always perked up at the mention drag races – his own baby, 1968 Camaro SS, was parked dutifully outside).

Eddie was pleased to go about his work, the same way he did

every Saturday, lullabied by the two of them talking, grateful they didn't take notice that he never joined in, never had anything to offer... The hum of their voices reassured him, and he felt a portion of something...

Soon enough, five minutes of eleven rolled around, and Curtis bellowed out the usual line to his small crew.

"Okay, people... let's get ready for another Fantastic day...!" and made for the steel-enforced, double- glass doors. Pulling a mess of keys from a long chain in his pocket, he violently turned the lock of one door, then the other, each one giving with a loud 'snap'! Everyone, including most patrons of Chicken Fantastic, had wished those doors be propped wide open, rather than simply unlocked, the smell of grease was so great (especially in Summer time). As immune as you became to it, you never really became immune.

Statistically, the thing that set Chicken Fantastic apart from most other fast food restaurants, was that upon opening, there were customers already waiting, either at the door, or in their automobiles, stacked up, along the drive-thru – not so for this unique fried chicken chain...

As per usual for the first hour of every Saturday, Eddie, Sharon, and Curtis (Curtis doing as little as possible, he being manager) killed time, and kept busy, going from table to table, topping off already filled salt shakers, stuffing already stuffed paper napkin holders, and making sure there were full rolls of toilet paper upon the spools in the restrooms, which there were (though both Eddie and Sharon deferred to the other to mop the amenity).

Just before noon, the first customer came in – a housewife who was in her mid-forties, and who looked about twenty years older than that... She had her short brown hair in curlers, and wore an orange and yellow flowered cotton housecoat, that had four buttons that ran up the middle, and barely went above her knees... Pink house slippers, in place of shoes, were upon her feet... A rather heavy imitation leather purse hung, clutched by a strap in her hand.

She stopped a foot in front of the counter, tilting her head back, and scanned back and forth the overhead menu, of what Chicken Fantastic has to offer her world. Eddie looked at this woman, in her housecoat, looking like an advertisement for 'God knew what', and a stab of pain went through him, as he was reminded of his own mother at home, who at this very hour, was into her same routine, wearing very much the same garb as this woman, only glued to a television set, rather than venturing out of the house.

Sharon leaned against the counter, her beautiful black spandex clad tummy resting upon the backs of her folded hands.

"Hi. Welcome to Chicken Fantastic. Can I take your order..?" There was something surreal about all of this.

The woman ordered a rather large order (presumably for a large number of waiting people). Sharon relayed to Eddie, and he and Curtis got busy doing the grunt work; while she did the register. The woman in the housecoat kept busy at a table, with her smart phone, and an iced tea. Five minutes later, she had a Fantastic Bucket, and was out the door.

The worst part was getting into the rhythm of work, and productivity, and then coming to a dead halt again. The three of them had just built up a kinetic energy, a rhythm, and now found themselves looking at each other, with nothing to say...

Curtis, being the consummate manager that he was, jumped upon the opportunity of the lull. "Deysyk," he said. "Take your thirty, for lunch..."

Sharon immediately defended him. "Curtis, he can't eat now..! It's way too early..!"

Curtis stared back at her, answered sternly. "Who's the manager here, Komperda..?! Lunch is when I say it is..!" He broke off for a moment, his big face seeming, not exhausted, but exasperated, at having lost it's cool – especially at Sharon – but then went on, at both of them. "...You know, I'm pretty cool with you guys...I don't make you work that hard. I do some of this shit myself – a lotta' shit other managers would never even do..! If you come in late I don't care..."

As he was going on, it occurred to Eddie, not only had Curtis been saving this up for quite awhile, he had quite an inner life – it was obvious Curtis' feelings were hurt, and this overweight, slightly crude, twenty-eight year old, high school drop cut that Eddie saw in just this way, was forever changed in his eyes...

Curtis wrapped up, mostly directing at Sharon, which was fine, since Eddie really hadn't objected to an early lunch. "...Whenever you want to take off early on a Saturday night..." He stopped, focused on Sharon. "Sharon, are you leavin' early..?'

Sharon, who had been taking this with her hands on her hips, just glared back at him with a cat's defiance. Eddie thought she looked beautiful, like a movie starlet, from the days of black and white films. She said nothing for an answer. Curtis understood, and went on.

"Yeah, so... Whenever you want off early, I'm cool with that..." At this he started reeling himself back in; composing himself; as if someone who had forgotten what they were angry about to begin with. "...I'm just sayin', you guys... When I say something, I expect it to be done... I'm the manager here... If no one listens to me, this whole place falls apart..."

Curtis finished his speech, which seemed more like a practiced recital, and there was an awkward silence hanging in the air... The five months that Eddie had been on, it had been mostly just the three of them, working Saturday's – a cool, laid-back crew; never one word of frustration, or a log jam to speak of... But, to these two younger kids, this was just as job; but to Curtis – who was pushing thirty years of age – it wasn't funny anymore...

Sharon turned her beautiful blonde head soberly to Eddie. "Go sit down. I'll make you a basket..." she said. She was cool, that way. Chicken Fantastic was fantastic about providing complimentary meals for employees (one basket includes one leg, one breast, one biscuit, one small drink), but you had to punch out.

Instead, Sharon punched out for Eddie (as one usually did, when one would cook for the other), and Eddie grabbed a small Coke, and sat a sat table near the window... He watched this beautiful girl dutifully get to work on his 'Fantastic' lunch, and his mind drifted back to the first time he set eyes on Sharon Komperda... It was the very first day of high school – freshman year – sitting in the back of academic-level sociology class... There had been no assigned seating, and Eddie was grateful to grab a seat in the corner, back of the class... Everyone was seated, the bell rang, and fashionably-late, in slunk Sharon Komperda, sixteen years of sexually-experienced, devil-may-care, one of a kind; and Eddie Deysyk would not take his off her the entire semester...

By the end of the eighteen weeks, he had come to know everything there was about her – she had gone to Roosevelt Middle School; her boyfriend (from whom she was never separated) was Ritchie Fackerell... He was eight months her junior, but although they had met while in the seventh grade, they had become sexually active, and had been lovers ever since. Everyone at the high school thought their romance was 'just the bomb', and kept up with every developing detail. Eddie thought it was a miracle Sharon wasn't waddling through the halls, eight months pregnant. Eddie had second period P.E. with Ritchie Fackerell – they never spoke, but Eddie caught sight of him changing after class one period, and his dick was enormous... It was also uncircumcised.

So, besides that Sharon Komperda had a boyfriend of three years, and that they were madly in love, and they were schtupping, and that his dick was big, what else did he know of this elusive, mysterious girl, who was really a woman, long before she could drive..? Eddie knew she was really intelligent; quite possibly brilliant... The few times Mr. Stillwell would call on her for an answer, it was because he would indignantly catch her writing notes to Ritchie during one of his lectures.

"Miss Komperda..." (And he'd go on to ask the question).

There would be a thick silence in the class as all waited to see what the coolest, most desired chick would do or say... Indeed, Eddie's stare from the back of the room was immutable, as Sharon's reply was always perfect... She would regard Mr. Stillwell with not so much of a defiance as it was a tired contempt... She would take three or four long seconds to process the question, then provide the answer in her dumb, moll-like, 'girly' voice. Mr. Stillwell would take a second or two, himself, to weigh what she had said.

"That's right," he invariably said.

Then, perturbed no more, she would go back to writing her notes to Ritchie – all this while curled up in her chair like a cat.

Eddie sat at his table, sipping his Coke, and daydreamed away the first five minutes of his thirty-minute lunch... Curtis didn't know this; Sharon must never know; Eddie's Saturday evenings were filled escorting his mother up, and out of the house... Prying her firstly, away from the television set, and secondly, out of the brown bathrobe, and into a fresh dress, was priority...at least once a week...

Eddie wasn't ashamed of his life with his mother, as much as he would have been embarrassed; horribly so, if anyone had ever found out just how constrained things were in their home, how dependent she was upon him. He loved his mother, but had come to learn that all things in life are just themselves, and very much stood alone to be judged, no matter who or what, they were...

These Saturdays – working in a greasy, smelly, money-oriented, pit of a place – were his rainbow... These two co-workers (sometimes they varied, but these two were an absolute sunny day) were family, to him; young cousins that he ran away with across the fields, or swam with for hours, in some swimming hole...even if he mostly never said a word, and did all the listening... Here he escaped the drawn shades of the house, the television with the predictably same shows, and a mother he loved, and who had given up on herself...

Indeed, these Saturdays were his rainbow...

Sharon brought over his lunch – a Fantastic Basket (one leg, one breast, one biscuit, choice of small fries or mashes potatoes). Eddie preferred fries, though he always left them. His reason for doing so was a kind of silent protest against big corporations that exploited the poor masses, who were lacking in nutrition education, as much as they were lacking in money – national chicken chains, along with Chicken Fantastic, promoted themselves as being everybody's hero by offering two pieces of chicken, two sides, and a drink...but if you really looked, you were getting two ounces of meat; and over a quarter pound of starch...no greens, no fruit, whatsoever – these places didn't even offer them on the menu... So he ate his chicken; ate his biscuit; drank his Coke; and threw the rest away...

"Here Eddie" Sharon said, in her dangerous 'girly' voice. She slid a Fantastic Basket over to him. "I'm sorry about Curtis..." Referring to the manager's earlier eruption, that really had been at her instigation.

"That's alright, Sharon" Eddie said, simply, and took his food, but not without saying, "Thank you..."

Eddie was midway through his lunch, when the ringtone of the cell went off in his pocket. A sinking feeling began in his stomach, as he immediately knew who it was...

He looked at the screen, swiped it, to answer. "Hi, Ma..." He tried to sound pleasant.

"Hi, Eddie, teddy bear ..." His mother tried to sound enthusiastic, but more than anything, she sounded tired, and worn, from doing nothing with herself. He pictured her, on the other end, still in her bathrobe, in the dark house.

The sinking feeling completed itself; he mustered his words. "Whaddya' doin'?" Though he knew the answer.

"Oh," she came back, listless, "...lookin' at T.V...What are *you* doing...?"

Eddie's eyes rose up, as if from underwater, and he looked at his surroundings – Sharon was at the counter, changing money for a customer who had just walked in, and Curtis, was busy, preparing the order, his big belly swinging away, as he did so... Suddenly, Eddie realized the escape of these Saturdays – the stark contrast of the youth and vigor, of this place, and the hopelessness of the growing desperation, at home...

"I'm workin', Ma," he finally said, and was quiet.

"Am I taking my best guy out, tonight..?" Her attempt to put verve into her voice was infinitely painful for Eddie to hear – this good woman had been damaged, residually, by years, not only of neglect, but months and months of the routine, of doing nothing. Suddenly, Eddie hated his father, who was quick to send large sums of money ever month, but was never around; hated that his father would ask a quick, 'how's your mother?', when they spoke, and then get off the subject; hated that his father was never coming back...

"Yeah, Ma," he tried to sound cheerful. "We'll go out. As soon as I get home. I'll get changed, and we'll go..."

"Okay," she sounded small. "I love you, Eddie, teddy bear ..."

"I love you too, Ma..." He put the phone in the pocket of his white work shirt.

Ten minutes after speaking with his mother, Eddie was punched in, and back at work...twenty minutes after that, Chicken Fantastic was swamped... The deluge began the way all great mid-western thunderstorms do – a drop, here; a drop, there...

At first, an old man came in by himself, trembling from old age, peering up through thick-rimmed, fogged-up glasses, wanting only two pieces of chicken, and coleslaw... Then, on his heels, a mother came in, wanting a ten-piece meal (a Fantastic Bucket) and drinks – this got Eddie and Curtis hopping, tossing chicken parts, and chicken livers into the air; parts and livers mixed with Fantastic Flour, then tossed into the fryer; then passed off to Sharon, who in turn had already rung up the money...

Very efficient, but very surreal...

The storm, meanwhile, was picking up – two cars were stacked outside the drive-thru... It was Sharon's job, if she was available (luckily, she was), to take orders. She put a microphone/headgear over her beautiful blonde head, and winced.

"Auggh..!" she recoiled. "It smells..! Hi, Welcome to Chicken Fantastic, can I help you..?"

(She sounded like combination of an angel and a sexpot...)

She took the order, relayed it via computer to Eddie and Curtis; took the order for the car behind; relayed that one, as well...

Sweat rolled down Curtis' face – his long blonde hair, plastered to his broad forehead... Eddie heard him mumbling obscene words, under his breath, while his gigantic belly swung around, as he tried to keep up... Eddie was cool, but his ass was moving just as fast.

There were orders flying over the counter. Orders flying out the drive-thru. Fantastic Buckets. Fantastic Baskets. Fantastic Buckets *with* Fantastic Baskets. Soft drinks. Side orders. Finally, when all of this has subsided...no less than five adults, three children, three automobiles full of people, had gone...a fat kid in the restaurant portion spilled his large soft drink all over the floor. It went slaying, in a direction of five feet caramel and corn syrup, everywhere.

Sharon just froze, looking surreal, but beautiful, in her white uniform, and headgear – her beautiful green/blue eyes, locked on the fat kid, who was ridiculously holding the empty cup, in apology.

"I'm not cleaning that," she said. "That's all know..."

Curtis, who was by this point, a bit cooled down, stared almost vaguely at the boy. "I'll kill that fuckin' kid..." he said to no one in particular.

"I'll get it," Eddie said, and went around the counter, with the mop and bucket.

"*Stephen*!" The fat boy's mother was scolding. "Look what you did!" Apparently, the boy's mother had been using the ladies restroom, and been unaware of her son's misfortune. Well, as they were now the only two occupants of Chicken Fantastic, the spilled drink was unavoidable. She grabbed his big arm, whirled him around, paddling him, three times...

The boy just winced, as if he was used to this.

"It's alright, ma'am..." Eddie ventured. "We get this all the time..." he smiled.

The mother, still clutching her son's arm, just regarded Eddie with wan look, saying nothing... After a moment she looked down at her son, and said, "Come on, Stephen."

The two left Eddie to clean up...

The Universe has a history, from the beginning of time, at least since the beginning of fast-food service, that everything comes in waves (winning-streaks, happiness, chart-topping success, for music groups) – this is no less true for Saturday's at Chicken Fantastic... The deluge ended – the irate mother, and her clumsy, fat son had cleared the place, and it was just the three of them, again... The intense smell of grease hung thickly in the air...

Curtis mopped the sweat from his face, slammed a large paper cup against the soft drink machine, poured himself a Coke, and sat himself at a window seat.

"Sharon" he said. "Take your lunch..."

"I have to call Ritchie," she said, dutifully, removing the microphone/headgear, and Eddie felt a familiar jealous flush – for as long as he had worked a shift with Sharon Komperda, she forsook each and every lunch break, to bring what would otherwise be her lunch, out to Ritchie Fackerell, who drove his piece of shit, out-dated Lincoln Continental, to meet her... Her half hour was spent in the front seat of his rusted out whale of a car; *he* eating free food, *she* being in love... Eddie was jealous. Eddie was powerless.

Sharon went to make the chicken pieces for Ritchie's Fantastic Basket; dropped them into the fryer. She deep fried his order of fries. As per every time he came by, she would wait until he arrived, to make his soft drink...

In reality, Sharon would go on to marry her high school sweetheart, and not only would their romance endure the bounds of high school, they go on to have many children together (eventually losing one to a long illness) – this small-town, one-in-a-million sexpot, with a quirky voice, proved to be quite an uncommon woman of character...

"Sit down, Deysyk." Curtis beckoned, from his window booth. "I've had it with this place, for awhile..."

Eddie thought reflectively, for a moment, then went over to join Curtis, opposite him, at a table. Curtis had already brought two large Cokes for them to enjoy, for their much-deserved break... As Eddie sat down, it occurred to him, how Curtis' large belly barley fit – seemed stuffed – between the table and accommodating bench.

"Fuckin' unbelievable..!" Curtis said, jiggling ice, in his soda cup. "When it rains, it pours..."

"I can't believe how busy it was," Eddie said; by now he was trying to inconspicuously keep track of Sharon, who herself was finishing Ritchie's Fantastic Basket – any moment, he would be pulling up in his out-dated clunker, for his free meal, and soda...

"You're sweet on her, ain't you..?"

The voice, only half-heard, came while Eddie was daydreaming, watching Sharon, so he didn't hear. Eddie snapped his head around to meet Curtis' gaze, to ask him what he had said, pretty sure he had heard correctly. "I'm sorry, what did you say..?"

"You heard me, Deysyk... I said you're sweet on her, ain't you..?"

Eddie felt the color drain from out of his face, and the cold, as his hands wrapped around the paper soft drink cup. "No I'm not..!" was all he could come up with to say, and hoped his response was fast enough.

"Yeah..." Curtis said, sizing him up, still jiggling his ice. "You're sweet on that chick..! It's cool, though...everybody wants to fuck her... Personally, I think half the time, she wants to fuck herself..."

Eddie didn't know what to say to all of this, so he looked at Sharon, who by this time had brought her boyfriend's lunch to the other side of the counter, who by this time had himself had arrived, and was waiting outside. Eddie felt his usual flush of anger, as he watched this beautiful, mysterious girl, rush out the door, to dote upon this seemingly unappreciative jerk...

"You have somebody, Deysyk?" Curtis' voice came out of nowhere, as much as his question seemed to, as well. Eddie regarded Curtis with clarity, clutching his soda, blinked twice...

"...I sort of take care of my mom..." he said.

Curtis just looked at him for a moment, processing this; after this moment, said, "Oh...it's like that..." But he said it in a way, as if he suddenly understood everything about Eddie – why he was so quiet; kept to himself; rarely socialized outside of work and school.

"My dad left a while ago... so it's just us, now..."

Curtis did more processing, sipped more soda. He took a deep breath, his giant belly heaving, looked straight at Eddie, and said, "Don't worry, man – you'll find someone..."

This was again, an unexpected remark, and Eddie didn't quite know how to respond; although he one hundred percent understood where Curtis was coming from, and what he meant. Although Eddie felt himself sinking, he managed to say, "I'll be alright..."

"Seriously, man," Curtis went on. "You'll find someone... Most people who are together are for the sake of convenience... Sure, when they first get together, it's right on, and everything, but after awhile, you realize it's just routine...and basically...it's a big scary world out there, and not only is it convenient, but nobody wants to go back to being alone."

Eddie thought about this for a moment, looked at Curtis. "Is that true..?"

"Man..!" Curtis went on, enthusiastically. "Most people who are in a relationship wait until their loyalty or (and for this he brought his finger up to exclamate his point) quote unquote love, is tested... That's when you realize, my friend, that what you think is two people "in love", is really just two people who "want one another"...

Curtis finished his speech, kept looking at Eddie. "Comprende..?!"

Eddie was silent, still looking at Curtis; still clutching his soda. "I think so..." he said.

Curtis nodded his head, to look out the restaurant, but he kept addressing Eddie. "...See those two, out there...?"

Eddie turned his head, to look where Curtis was looking – at Ritchie and Sharon, sitting in the front seat of Ritchie's shit-box... He could make out the tops of their heads; Sharon's blonde one, Ritchie's auburn... They were long since ensconced in their own little world. The sinking feeling that Eddie regularly felt every Saturday, at this time, sank one degree lower.

"Those two," Curtis said, matter of factly, "are going to be together forever... In fact, they probably knew each other in some past life... They'll probably meet each other *again*...!"

Eddie was transfixed by Curtis' words.

"That's just the way it is with the world... The world needs real lovers; to keep it turning... Give it meaning... Comprende..?!"

"Yes," Eddie said, but he felt small within himself; humbled by what he had heard, and a reverence for Sharon and Ritchie.

"Life is more than Chicken Fantastic..." Curtis finished, and summed up, by finishing his Coke. "Just take care of your mom, man... Being a friend to her your best bet..."

Eddie felt a wave of confidence and warmth rise up within him – not only was he now looking at Curtis in a way he had never before seen him, no one had ever spoken to Eddie in quite such a way.

Eddie turned his head, one more time to look at Ritchie and Sharon – they were in the front seat of Ritchie's rusted-out behemoth, turned intimately toward one another. Their lips moved, as they spoke words only young lovers understood. No one could know, but in less than five years time, both would be married to one another (with a wedding for which they, themselves would pay), go on to have three children, lose one to fatal illness, and survive divorce.

Five minutes later, Eddie and Curtis were back behind the counter. No one had as yet come in, and the only sound in the place was the constant rejuvenation of the imitation Hawaiian-coconut drink machine, as its contents swirled endlessly around, keeping it fresh, for the next poor soul.

When her thirty minutes were up, the doors opened, and Sharon came in, walking her defiant, feline walk... Curtis was quick to notice her energy.

"You and Ritchie smoke a little something, out there..?" he asked, coyly.

Eddie looked at her; and to the casual observer, you wouldn't have seen it, but to the discerning eye, you could see the girl was stoned – her eyes were reddish around the rims, and her beautiful face was now distantly straining to concentrate, since being disturbed by Curtis.

She looked at him like a cat whose sleep has been disturbed. "I did *not*...!" she almost hissed.

"Yeah," he started to play with her. "You're stoned." Curtis turned to Eddie, consulted him. "Isn't she stoned, Dyesyk?"

Sharon turned her head to look at Eddie, clearly tired of being ganged up on, and Eddie didn't appreciate being put on the spot, in such a way.

"I wouldn't know." He said, taking his eyes off of Sharon.

"She's high..." Curtis said, finally; playfully. "Komperda, get yourself something to eat; go sit down; take an extra ten minutes to get yourself together."

Sharon looked silently at him for a moment, and Eddie was aware of a telepathy that exchanged between the two – a special telepathy that evolved amongst the partiers, and the lovers, and the free of this world – one they used to communicate when they needed to depend upon one another in times of crises... Following this moment, Sharon silently grabbed a Fantastic Biscuit, fixed an iced tea with ice, and sat at a corner booth.

By now Curtis was working on the next week's schedule; upon the counter, in full view of whatever customers would chance to come in, rather than the office. His greasy blonde hair fell about his face, and upon his face, an almost comical look of consternation. He stopped wiggling his pencil in thought, and looked about, to see if customers were about.

"Hey. Deysyk..!" he called out. "Next Saturday. You want morning..?!"

Eddie didn't need two seconds to think about it. "Sure, Curtis" he said. "Thanks."

"Komperda..!" Curtis half-bellowed, across the restaurant. "Next Saturday. Same as today. Yes or No..?!"

Sharon, who clearly was yet a degree buzzed from her 'lunch hour' with her boyfriend, looked at Curtis a bit dazedly – distractedly – and nodded a 'yes'.

Curtis looked at her, half playfully – "Is that a 'yes'..?!"

Sharon met his stare. "Yeah." She managed, sternly, in her girly voice.

"Oh, and incidentally," Curtis addressed her. "That's your five minutes in 'La-La land' – get back to work."

For the remainder of the beautiful spring day, there were but a trickle of customers, on and off; and it was constantly a wonder how Chicken Fantastic managed to stay in business at all. Eddie gripped the counter, and waited on customers, throughout the day; but there was something cathartic about what had occurred today – he had come to realize an extra dimension within the people he worked with; an extra dimension within his mother, and what *she* was going through...

Perhaps he would give his father a chance at their relationship – he had but one father, and one chance at this... Tonight he would take his mother out to dinner, and they would talk about everything, and have a fine time. For now, he had a good head on his shoulders; a job three days a week; a car; and people in his life who loved him; and that was more than some; even most...

And he had Curtis and Sharon – his extended family, who he could count upon seeing most Saturdays; Curtis and Sharon, whose youth and vibrance he so very much looked forward to every week. Eddie Deysyk felt himself reassured, and reabsorbed within the bosom of an indefinite unfolding of Saturdays...

THE END